FESTIVAL READERS

George

COLUMBIA PICTURES PRESENTS A MARVEL ENTERPRISES PRODUCTION A LAURA ZISKIN PRODUCTION "SPIDER-MAN"
STARRING: TOBEY MAGUIRE   WILLEM DAFOE   KIRSTEN DUNST   JAMES FRANCO   CLIFF ROBERTSON   ROSEMARY HARRIS
MUSIC BY DANNY ELFMAN   EXECUTIVE PRODUCERS AVI ARAD   STAN LEE   SCREENPLAY BY DAVID KOEPP   BASED ON THE MARVEL COMIC BOOK BY STAN LEE   PRODUCED BY LAURA ZISKIN   IAN BRYCE   DIRECTED BY SAM RAIMI

MARVEL                                     sony.com/Spider-Man                                     COLUMBIA PICTURES

Library of Congress Catalog Card Number: 2001092288

6  7  8  9  10

❖

First Edition

www.harperchildrens.com
GO FOR THE ULTIMATE SPIN AT
www.sony.com/Spider-Man

# Spider-Man Saves the Day

*Adaptation by Acton Figueroa*

*Based on the screenplay by David Koepp*

*Illustrations by Ron Lim*

 HarperFestival®

*A Division of* HarperCollins*Publishers*

SPIDER-MAN

Being a superhero is different
than you might think.
It's exciting, that's for sure.
I get to swing through the city
and climb up buildings.

I can shoot webbing.

I can cling to walls.

I can sense when people
are in trouble.

But there's a lot more to it
than that.

At first I used my powers to have fun.

But then I remembered what Uncle Ben told me: "With great power comes great responsibility."

It was time for me to do something good for the people of this city.

This man runs the corner

grocery store.

He's been there for years.

All the kids buy candy

from him.

He's a nice man.

But bad guys will be bad guys.
One night somebody tried
to rob him.
The grocer was in big trouble.

I sensed there was a problem.

I came. I saw.

I aimed a big web-strand

at the robber.

The problem was solved.

One night a couple of guys decided to rob a jewelry store. It didn't take long for me to wrap things up.

I hate to see anyone in trouble. But I get really angry when I see someone I like getting pushed around.

My superpowers come in handy at times like this.

People began to wonder
about the amazing Spider-Man
who was fighting crime—
and winning—in their city.
The newspapers wrote
about the new web-spinning,
wall-climbing superhero.
Everyone wanted to know
who I was.

I don't usually take credit
for the good deeds I do.

Courtesy,
your friendly

neighborhood

SPIDER-MAN.

But sometimes
I can't help myself.

Some people think I'm crazy
to do what I do.
It is dangerous.

And some people think

I might be dangerous, too.

People can think
whatever they want.

I have a job to do, and I do it.

Knowing I've helped someone
is all the reward I need.

Some people have the wrong

idea about me . . .

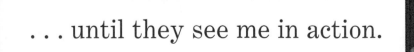

. . . until they see me in action.

This is the best part of my job.

Whenever someone in this city
needs me, I'll be there.

You can be sure of that.

I'm your friendly neighborhood
Spider-Man!